STANDING TALL
Mystery
S e r i e s

RL 3.9

MULTICULTURAL READERS
SET 1

✓ P9-CCI-173

DON'T LOOK
NOW OR EVER

ANNE SCHRAFF

🏠 Artesian Press

P.O. Box 355 Buena Park, CA 90621

STANDING TALL MYSTERY SERIES
MULTICULTURAL READERS
SET 1

Project Editor: Carol E. Newell
Cover Illustrator: TSA Design Group
Cover Design: Tony Amaro
©2000 Artesian Press

ISBN 1-58659-084-7

Chapter 1

Jennifer Diaz's science teacher said everybody had to watch the moon each night and keep track of the phases. That was why Jennifer was looking out the window at 8:30 P.M. She noted that the moon was full. Then her gaze dropped to the street below. She sucked in her breath in horror to see two boys fighting hand-to-hand. One of them had a knife that flashed in the moonlight.

Santiago Velasquez and Artur Sandoval were never friends, but now they fought savagely like bitter enemies. Suddenly Santiago was on his knees. Jennifer put her hands to her face, a scream frozen in her throat. It was like watching a horror movie as Santiago crawled down the sidewalk and Artur sprinted away.

Jennifer knew she should call 911 at once, but then they would have her name and address. Bad things sometimes happened to witnesses in this neighborhood.

Jennifer continued to stare out the window a moment after both boys were gone. Was Santiago badly injured? Had he crawled somewhere bleeding? Jennifer threw down her Science book and ran from the apartment, down the stairs to the street. She went to the pay phone on the corner and dashed in, dialing 911. "I saw two boys fighting at 21st and Hawthorne. Maybe one was knifed. You'd better come quick," Jennifer blurted before hanging up quickly.

Now the police only had the address of the pay phone. They could not trace the call to the Diaz house. Jennifer paused in front of the furniture store where the boys had been fighting.

She couldn't help but notice the blood stain on the sidewalk, and she shuddered, running back upstairs as fast as she could.

Jennifer knew both boys, but neither was a friend. They argued a lot with each other, but neither of them seemed really bad. Both were on the East Tech basketball team. Santiago was the better player. He was also the handsomest, but he had a short fuse. Artur made better grades. His older brother was in prison. It was the great sorrow of the family.

Jennifer was breathing hard when she reached her room. She didn't want to be anywhere near that bloodstained sidewalk when the police arrived.

"You've been outside, Jen?" Dad asked from the living room. "Heard the door slam."

"Yeah, I've got to look at the moon for my Science class," Jennifer yelled back. In a few minutes the wail of a police siren filled the air. An ambulance came, too, and the corner filled up with police and paramedics in search of a wounded boy. Jennifer was looking out the window when her mother came alongside her.

"What's going on down there?" Mom asked.

"I don't know," Jennifer said. "Maybe an accident." She was still trembling, so she folded her arms to steady herself.

"Oh, I hope it's nothing bad," Mom said. "Say a prayer that nobody is hurt."

Jennifer closed her eyes and the faces of the two boys came to mind. Santiago liked to needle the other guys on the basketball team, especially Artur. In the last big game Artur scored more points than Santiago, usually the big scorer in every game. Santiago really got on Artur for that. He thought Artur put him in the shade. He didn't like it.

"Must be something serious," Dad said, joining them at the window, "there's another police car."

Jennifer felt numb. Maybe she'd been the only witness to a terrible crime!

Chapter 2

The police remained for about forty-five minutes and then left. Nobody had been put in the ambulance when they drove away too. Jennifer breathed a sigh of relief. Probably Santiago and Artur just traded a few punches and one of them got a nosebleed. Maybe the knife that flashed in the moonlight wasn't a knife at all—maybe it was somebody's metal watch band.

Jennifer smiled a little. She did have a vivid imagination. Her older brother, Martin, always said she could make something out of nothing. "If there's a lizard in the yard, you see the return of the dinosaurs! A plane is a flying saucer, *mi hermana!*" he said.

Jennifer finished her homework and tried to forget what she'd seen in the darkness. The next morning she walked to East Tech with her friend, Alma Nuanes. Alma lived on the next block.

"Did you hear all the sirens last night, Jen?" Alma asked. "They sounded like they were on your street."

"Yeah," Jennifer said, "some police cars and an ambulance came, but I guess it was a false alarm."

"I worried maybe it was a gang fight," Alma said.

Jennifer said nothing. She didn't want to talk about it to anybody. It was her own overreacting that caused the false alarm. Probably because of her call the city spent a lot of money they couldn't afford.

"Big game Friday, huh?" Alma said. "Tyler High is coming over. Our big rivals. Everybody is real excited. I hope Santiago is hot, 'cause we need every point. Lately he's been dragging his tail.

Tyler is going to be looking for revenge because we beat them so bad at their school, you know."

Jennifer didn't like basketball as much as Alma did. Jennifer got a lot more excited on a Science field trip learning how to make thick green lather from Buffalo Gourd plants than she did at a game.

Artur was in Jennifer's first class, Science. She was anxious to see him, just to make sure he was acting natural. Surely if something horrible had happened last night he wouldn't come to school as usual.

As Jennifer walked into class she saw Artur in his usual spot, near the front. He liked to sit close to the teacher so he could hear and take good notes. Artur had to work hard to make decent grades. When Artur turned towards Jennifer she saw that he had a black eye, and she shuddered.

"Where'd you get that shiner, man?"

a boy asked.

"Where everybody gets 'em, running into a door," Artur answered, and everybody laughed.

"Did you run into some guys from Tyler?" another boy asked. "If they roughed you up, we'll even the score for you, Artur."

"Nah," Artur said, "it really was a stupid door."

Jennifer couldn't concentrate during Science. She wouldn't rest easy until she saw Santiago on campus. She didn't share any classes with him, but she always saw him coming out of Basic Math with his friend, Davis Watson. He was also a fine basketball player.

But when Basic Math let out, Davis was alone.

"Hey, Davis," Jennifer said, "where's Santiago?"

Davis shrugged. "Don't know," he said. "Maybe he ditched."

"He doesn't ditch much," Jennifer

said nervously. "Coach kicks guys off the team for that."

A few minutes later Jennifer saw Luci Loperena, Santiago's girlfriend. "Hey Luci, do you know where Santiago is? He missed his Math class," Jennifer said.

"That's not all he missed," Luci snapped, her dark eyes flashing, "he missed our date last night, too!"

Chapter 3

"You guys had a date for last night?" Jennifer asked.

"Yeah. I get off work at the donut shop at 9, and he was supposed to pick me up. We were going for hamburgers. He never showed! I waited an hour for him. Then I had to call my Dad to come get me. He was as mad as a bear jerked out of hibernation!" Luci fumed. "And the worst part is, Santiago didn't even call to say he was sorry!"

Jennifer struggled to concentrate in her next class. She didn't like English anyway, but today it was unbearable. It was the longest class period of Jennifer's life.

At lunchtime, Jennifer called the

Velasquez home. Maybe Santiago was home nursing a bruise from the fight, and he was embarrassed to show himself. He was very vain about his appearance, so an ugly bump on his face would have freaked him out.

The phone at the Velasquez home rang and rang. Jennifer knew that Santiago lived with his father and he was often gone on business trips, but where was Santiago? If he wasn't at school, he should be home.

Jennifer desperately wanted to share her terrible secret with somebody, but she didn't dare. If she told Alma that she had witnessed the boys having a terrible fight in the street, Alma would spill the beans. Alma's mother was on the neighborhood watch program, and she was very brave and public spirited. But Jennifer was afraid. When Jennifer was only seven her cousin was almost killed when men fired shots at her house. They mistakenly believed someone in the house had reported them to the police. That frightening incident remained in Jennifer's mind. She could remember tracing the spot near her cousin's bed where the bullets had ripped into the wall.

When Jennifer saw Artur after school she said, "Santiago missed school today."

"So?" Artur said. He seemed very nervous.

"I uh … just wondered. He's a teammate and stuff." Jennifer mumbled. "I thought he was sick and told you or something."

Artur came closer to Jennifer. His face was shiny with perspiration. Jennifer had never seen him like that before, not even during thé games. "I don't know anything about him. Maybe he decided to ditch school and move to Brazil. I don't even like the guy. Why should I care where he is?" he said in a tense voice.

"Okay, okay," Jennifer said, hurrying away. She went home. Later that evening, she called Santiago's house again. The phone rang as before without an answer. Jennifer desperately wanted to know where Santiago was, but she couldn't make unusual inquiries. That would focus attention on her.

Jennifer decided to call Alma and beat around the bush for an answer. Alma was such a basketball fan that she knew more about the players than Jennifer did.

"Alma, I'm really worried that Santiago won't make the game Friday," Jennifer lied. "I even called his house and nobody answered. If he was sick or something, wouldn't he be home?"

"I think his father went to New York on a business trip," Alma said. "Santiago told me something about that."

"Maybe Santiago went with him," Jennifer said hopefully.

Alma laughed. "Oh, no. His father is a real fanatic about school. He would never let Santiago skip. And what about the game? Santiago is living for that game against Tyler. Tell you what, Jennifer, I'll ask my sister to drive me over there—to Santiago's apartment— and see what's going on."

Jennifer waited at the phone for an hour before Alma called back. "This is so weird—Santiago's place is locked tight. There's nobody home!"

Chapter 4

"Are you sure?" Jennifer asked.

"Yeah. We even asked the landlady. She said Santiago's Dad left on his business trip two days ago, and Santiago was there until last night. He left the house about 8 P.M. He just never showed up again." Alma said.

Jennifer thought she was going to be sick. It was about 8:30 when she saw the fight. And now it appeared that Santiago *had never gone home*.

After she hung up the phone, Jennifer searched her mind wildly for what to do. If she called the police and reported what she saw, they would arrest Artur. Artur would know what she had done. His friends would know. If something dreadful had happened to Santiago, then Jennifer would be the most important witness. She would be the one giving testimony to send Artur to prison like his brother.

Jennifer cried herself to sleep, hoping against hope that Santiago would show up at school tomorrow. He had done crazy, impulsive things before. Once he drove to Mexico without telling anybody and was gone for three days. His father was so angry he threatened to send Santiago to live with his mother and her husband, but Santiago only laughed. His mother didn't want him living with her, and everybody knew it.

Coach Randall was furious when Santiago didn't show up the next day. "That kid picked a heckuva time to pull a disappearing act," Coach Randall stormed. "Without him in the game we're doomed on Friday."

The baseball coach shook his head

and said, "He might be just making you sweat, Randall. He's a weird kid."

Jennifer was walking behind the two coaches when she suddenly blurted it out. "Uh ... I overheard some guys talking ... I forget who the guys were ... but they said Santiago was in a fight with another guy the night before last. Maybe there's nothing to it, but..."

Coach Randall's face turned very serious, "When was this fight?"

"Oh, you know, night before last. I just overheard these guys talking. They uh ... said Santiago and Artur were fighting." Jennifer said. Her lower lip was quivering so much she almost bit herself.

"Artur Sandoval?" Coach Randall asked.

"I guess," Jennifer said. "Uh ... don't mention my name, okay. I mean, I don't want to get mixed up in anything."

"Don't worry about it, Jennifer,"

Coach Randall said. "Nobody will get you involved. Thanks for the tip."

The two coaches' steps quickened. By afternoon it was all over school that Artur Sandoval had been pulled out of History to go to the principal's office.

"What do you think it's about?" Alma asked.

"Who knows?" Jennifer muttered.

After school, as Jennifer headed home, she saw Artur getting on his motorcycle. She avoided meeting his gaze until he called out, "Jennifer!"

"Oh, no," Jennifer whispered to herself, "he knows. *Somehow* he knows!" But she said nothing to Artur as he approached her.

"A funny thing happened to me today," Artur said. "I was called into the office, and they asked me a lot of questions about Santiago being missing and stuff. Like I knew something about it."

"Wow," Jennifer said, fighting to appear cool.

"Yeah. Coach Randall had some crazy story about some guys saying me and Santiago were in a big fight or something," Artur said. His gaze seemed to be drilling into Jennifer's brain. She wanted to scream. "Uh … Jennifer, you live over on Hawthorne in that big apartment near the corner, don't you?"

"Uh huh," Jennifer said.

"Were you home Tuesday night?" Artur asked.

"N-no," Jennifer said quickly. "I was visiting my Grandmother until about 10:30. Why?"

Artur smiled. "Oh, no reason. I just wondered."

Chapter 5

Jennifer was hurrying towards home when Luci Loperena caught up to her. "Hey Jen. Did you hear what happened at school today? They questioned Artur Sandoval about Santiago being gone and everything," she said.

"Yeah," Jennifer said. "I'll bet you're worried about him, huh, Luci ... about Santiago, I mean."

"Not really. We went out a few times, but he had a mean streak. I never could've loved him or anything. Like he'd really hassle Artur about his brother—the one who's in jail. Artur and his whole family was just so ashamed when the brother went to jail, and Santiago would like, get pictures of

Artur's brother from old yearbooks and draw striped jail clothes on him," Luci said.

"Oh," Jennifer said.

"Yeah. If Artur did something to Santiago it'd be because of stuff like that. Santiago seems to know just where you hurt the most, and that's what he strikes. Like with me, I'm kinda sensitive about my front teeth being a little crooked. And he'd call me 'snaggle-tooth'. He'd be laughing when he said it, but he knew it got to me, but he wouldn't stop."

"Why did you go out with him at all if he's like that?" Jennifer asked.

Luci shrugged. "I'm not exactly the prom queen, Jen. He asked me out, and I was flattered. He's an athlete. He's good looking. I think he asked me out so he could make me squirm with those snaggle-tooth jokes. But still it was fun being with a guy on Friday night instead of renting a movie and getting a jumbo bag of popcorn ... I guess it meant a lot to me just to be able to be seen with a date ... for once in my life!"

Luci and Jennifer went their separate ways at the corner. Jennifer walked on alone, remembering how she learned that Artur's brother had been arrested. She was a freshman when it happened. Artur said his brother was innocent, that he was framed. Jennifer didn't know if that was true or not, but she did know Artur was crushed.

"My brother will be in prison," he groaned. "In prison! That must be the most awful thing in the world. I'd rather be dead than be in prison."

Artur's mother began wearing black as if her oldest son had died, and the family stopped taking part in almost everything. Jennifer's mother and Artur's mother belonged to a club at church, but Artur's mother never showed up anymore.

Jennifer had an English assignment that evening, and she tried to work on it. Both her parents were working late tonight, so she jumped when the doorbell rang. She went to the door and peeked out to see a delivery boy with flowers. Jennifer closed the peep hole and said to the boy, "Just leave them, thank you."

Jennifer brought the flowers in then. There was a lovely white wicker basket full of red and white carnations. The little white card said, *Jenny—want to go for pizza with me after the game Friday? Artur.*

Jennifer put the basket on the table and stared at it. Artur was a nice boy, and if nothing else had happened, Jennifer would have accepted his offer. But now the offer made chills go up and down her spine.

Artur must suspect she had seen the fight in the darkness on that moonlit night. This was his way of trying to buy her silence.

"What's that?" Mom asked when she got home and saw the flowers. "Somebody must like my little girl a lot!"

Jennifer shook her head. "No, it's ... it's like he wants a favor, and this is his way of asking." she said.

"It must be a pretty big favor," Mom said, looking at the expensive flowers.

"Yeah," Jennifer said, continuing to look at the flowers. The last time she'd seen such a beautiful floral arrangement it had been at a funeral.

Chapter 6

On Thursday morning Jennifer told Artur she couldn't even come to the game. She told him she had to baby-sit her niece. It was a lie. She was lying all the time now, and she hated it. Ever since that terrible night when she looked out the window she had to lie. If only her teacher hadn't given that stupid assignment to watch the phases of the moon! Then she wouldn't have been looking out the window and maybe would not have seen Artur kill Santiago!

"I'm sorry you can't come," Artur said as they stood at the lockers at school. His gaze dropped to Jennifer's shell necklace. "Did you make that?"

"Yeah. Ages ago. I like to make

things," Jennifer said, She felt uncomfortable with him looking at her.

"I'll bet you'd look good in pearls," Artur said. "Your skin color is perfect for pearls."

"I don't like expensive stuff,- Jennifer said.

"Hey, Jennifer," Artur said, "did I ever tell you about my brother Luis?"

Jennifer shook her head.

"He's a good guy—a really good big brother. He's going to make something of himself when he gets out of prison. He's taking all kinds of courses, and he'll like have a college degree— almost," Artur said. Perspiration made his face shiny.

"That's good," Jennifer said, wishing the bell would ring so she wouldn't have to talk to Artur any longer.

"Yeah. He's getting out next year. He was doing five to ten. He's getting an early release because he is innocent," Artur said.

"Oh," Jennifer said.

"It was self defense, Jennifer. He killed a guy, but it was self defense. He shouldn't have been sent to prison at all," Artur said. "It's not a crime to defend your own life." His dark eyes were intense. His lips trembled. Jennifer had the feeling he wasn't describing the incident that got his brother in trouble at all. He was talking about what happened between him and Santiago. "You believe like that too, don't you, Jennifer? I mean a guy shouldn't go to prison for defending his own life."

"No, he shouldn't," Jennifer agreed, sprinting away at the bell, ice cold perspiration running down her body. Artur had all but admitted hurting Santiago. He was begging for her silence.

Jennifer was the only one who saw the fight! She wasn't sure who started it, who pulled the knife. Did Santiago try to hurt Artur, and then did Artur turn the knife against his attacker? Jennifer saw Santiago fall, and she was almost sure he was looking up at her window, perhaps seeing her face in the window. That face—Santiago's stricken face—haunted Jennifer. It was as if he was asking her to do her duty, to make sure justice was done. But how could she?

Even if Jennifer told the police what she saw, it wouldn't be enough to convict Artur. It would only be enough to make Artur and his friends hate her. They would be there in school with her, walking to the lockers with her, waiting for her after school.

On Friday, Jennifer was called out of her Science class and told to report to the principal's office. When she got there she saw Coach Randall and a police officer.

"I'm sorry, Jennifer," Coach Randall said, "but I had to mention your name to the police. I told them what you told me. I promise you that whatever you tell the police will go no farther than this room."

Jennifer sat down opposite a police lieutenant with short, curly hair. "I'm Lieutenant Emily Foster, Jennifer," she said. "I want you to tell me all you know about overhearing details of a fight between Santiago and Artur. It's very important that you talk to us, Jennifer, because we may be dealing with a homicide here."

"You mean you found Santiago's body!" Jennifer almost screamed. All the silly little paintings on the office walls swam together in a wild blur of color before her eyes.

Chapter 7

"No," Lt. Foster said, "but on the night Santiago Velasquez disappeared we received an anonymous phone call about two boys fighting at 21st and Hawthorne. We played the recording of that call, and Mr. Randall believes it's your voice."

Coach Randall looked guilty. "I'm sorry, Jennifer," he said softly.

"I didn't see anything," Jennifer said.

"But you did make the call that night, correct?" Lt. Foster asked crisply.

"Yes," Jennifer said. "I looked out the window at the moon for a school project, and then I saw these shadows fighting and one of them dropped and the other one sort of ran away."

"And you couldn't identify either person?" Lt. Foster asked. Her gaze seemed to drill into Jennifer like a laser beam.

"No," Jennifer lied. "It was too dark."

"Are you sure, Jennifer?" Lt. Foster asked.

"Yes, I'm sure," Jennifer snapped.

"You're very frightened, aren't you, Jennifer?" Lt. Foster said in a gentle voice. "You know, if you saw something and had to involve one of your fellow students, you'd receive police protection."

"I didn't see anything," Jennifer cried. "May I go now? I'm missing all my Science class, and I'm not good in there anyway. I don't want to flunk."

"Yes, you may go, Jennifer, but if you remember anything, just call me at this number," Lt. Foster said, handing Jennifer a card.

Jennifer walked back to Science and got in for the last ten minutes. As she left class, Alma grabbed her arm and whispered, "What was *that* all about? Did the cops talk to you?"

Jennifer shrugged. "They got this crazy idea I know something about where Santiago is. They ..." Tears ran down Jennifer's face, and she broke from Alma and ran across the school campus to the street. She couldn't be here anymore. She couldn't just go to classes as if nothing was wrong. Artur would know that the police talked to her. He would think she had betrayed him. She couldn't face him—she couldn't!

Jennifer ran down the street and ducked into a pay phone. She stuffed coins into the little slot. Her brother, Martin, lived across town in an apartment near his work.

"Marty," Jennifer sobbed into the phone, "it's me! I'm in big trouble! I'm at Tommy's Taco Stand."

"You're not hurt are you, little sister?" Martin asked.

"No ... oh, Marty it's just that ..."

"I'll be over in thirty minutes," Martin promised.

When Martin Diaz' old yellow bug pulled up in front of the taco stand, Jennifer raced towards it. She yanked the door open and fell into Martin's arms. In five seconds she told him everything.

"I remember Santiago Velasquez," Martin said. "He was in fourth grade the year I started East Tech. He was a mean little cuss even then. His parents got him a puppy for Christmas. He didn't like it, so he just dumped it on the street to fend for itself."

"Marty, do you think Artur killed Santiago?" Jennifer asked.

Martin thought for a moment, then he shook his head. "I never took Artur for a violent guy, but who knows what might have happened between them?'

"I saw them fighting, Marty ... I'm probably the only one who can put Artur there at the scene. Marty, I'm so scared. What will I do? Maybe I'm covering up for a murderer, but I'm too scared to tell!"

Chapter 8

"Let's just drive over to where it happened," Martin said. It was a short drive to 21st and Hawthorne. Jennifer and Martin got out of the car and walked to the spot where Jennifer had seen the boys fighting. "Now," Martin said carefully, "if Santiago was seriously hurt—you say he sort of crawled away. Where could he have crawled to? Maybe down that alley."

"When I looked again they were both gone," Jennifer said. "Maybe Artur followed Santiago to ... you know, finish him off."

"But what happened to Santiago or his body?" Martin asked. "Artur doesn't have a car. I'm sure he's not going to drag a dead guy several miles down the street to the river!"

They walked down the alley. Some of the stores that backed up on the alley had been vacant for a long time. A deep shudder ran through Jennifer's body as she looked at the broken back doors and the graffiti.

"Maybe he's in *there*," Jennifer said, seeing a door ajar. Martin pushed the door open more and stared in. Jennifer gasped to see a pile of debris over in one corner. Maybe Santiago crawled into a pile of burlap bags and just— died!

Martin led the way into the empty store. Jennifer followed, holding tightly to his arm.

"Blood stains," Martin said, looking at the floor.

"Marty!" Jennifer cried.

Martin shifted the debris with an old curtain rod and a mouse scurried across the floor. There was nothing under the burlap sacks. "Maybe Santiago came in here and made a bandage out of some of these rags, then went on," he said.

"But where would he have gone?" Jennifer asked.

"He has a car. Maybe it was parked around here," Martin said. "Let's say the guys came here to settle a score and when Santiago got hurt, he just ran away in his car."

"But wouldn't he have gone to a hospital?" Jennifer asked.

"Maybe he didn't make it," Martin said.

"And he's like parked somewhere in his car..." Jennifer said. Maybe he drove into some side street and nobody paid any attention to the car. Who pays attention to abandoned cars?

Martin drove around with Jennifer for a while looking for Santiago's blue sedan, but they saw no sign of it.

"Marty, what will I do?" Jennifer

wailed.

Martin pulled up in front of Jennifer's apartment. "Well," he said, "the police already suspect Artur. They're watching him, Jen. I don't think you have to say anything. Just keep cool and avoid Artur. After all, you don't really know much more than the police know."

Jennifer hugged her brother before she got out of the car. "I wish you still lived with us, Marty. I miss you!" she said.

"I miss you, too, *mi hermana*," Martin said. "Next year we're all going to take a vacation together to the Grand Canyon, right?"

"You bet," Jennifer said.

Jennifer went up to the apartment and let herself in. She collapsed on the couch in the living room. Then the phone rang. "Jenny," Alma cried excitedly, "where'd you go? I've been looking all over school for you! I thought maybe he'd gotten you, too!"

"I just couldn't take it anymore," Jennifer said.

"Everybody's saying they found Santiago's body," Alma said. "Everybody's saying Artur killed Santiago, and now the police have Santiago's body."

Jennifer turned numb. "Where did they find it?" she asked shakily.

"All kinds of rumors, Jenny," Alma said breathlessly. "One guy says they found him in a ditch and another said he was in a dumpster. Another thing too, Jenny. They're saying you can nail Artur 'cause you saw the thing happen. Did you, Jenny?"

Chapter 9

"No!" Jennifer shouted, slamming down the phone. She sat trembling in the darkened apartment for a few minutes. Then she headed for the kitchen to start dinner. Her parents wouldn't be home until the early evening and neither of them would be in the mood to make dinner.

Jennifer opened the kitchen door and then gasped.

"Artur!" she cried, seeing the boy at the stove.

"Don't be scared, Jennifer," he said. "I know I shouldn't have just come into your apartment without asking, but I found your key in the flower pot by the door."

Jennifer began backing up. She had to get out of the apartment and quick.

"Please don't run away, Jennifer," Artur said. "I'm making dinner. I bought some chicken and vegetables, and I've made the best *pollo encasuela con legumbres* you ever tasted. Dad's a chef, you know. He taught me all his tricks. I'm going to be a great chef someday."

Jennifer continued backing up until Artur sprinted across the room and blocked her escape.

"Please let me go," Jennifer said.

"Jennifer, I just want to talk to you for a little bit, okay?" Artur asked, leaning against the only door that led into the hall.

"I didn't tell the police anything about you when they talked to me," Jennifer said. Her heart was pounding wildly. She could scarcely breathe.

"What did you see from the window, Jennifer?" Artur asked. "Because

I saw you up there watching that night." Little beads of sweat sparkled on Artur's brow.

"Nothing—I saw nothing. I was watching the moon for a school project," Jennifer said. Her lower lip trembled so much she almost bit her tongue.

"You saw us, me and Santiago—you saw us fighting. He was always needling me about my jailbird brother and making snide remarks, cutting things. We decided to have it out, with fists. I wanted to fight him like a man. But I was getting the best of him, so he pulled a knife, somehow he got cut. I didn't cut him. I guess he cut himself or something. I got scared and ran. When I looked back he was gone. I figured he ran away, too ... but then I figured maybe he was cut bad and he ... you know ... died or something, 'cause where is he?"

Jennifer just stared at the boy.

"It all happened so fast. Like in some crazy movie, Jennifer. I don't know ... when he got cut he said, 'Now, you're gonna sweat you little scum.', like it was my fault. I just wonder where he is," Artur said.

Jennifer remembered what Alma said, that they'd found Santiago's body. All Jennifer knew was that she had to somehow get away from Artur.

"Let me go now, Artur," Jennifer said. "You've got to let me go."

He took a step towards her. "Don't you see what's happening, Jennifer? It's going to happen with me like it happened with my brother!" A terrible look gripped his face. "I'll be accused of something I didn't do. It's not right, Jennifer. They'll send me to prison just like they sent Luis—for something he didn't do. It's gonna be the end of my parents if that happens. I mean, they went through so much with Luis."

"I won't say anything, I swear," Jennifer said. "Just let me go."

"I didn't bring the knife—he did! Maybe he fell on it or something, but I didn't do anything," Artur was almost screaming now.

Jennifer heard a car stop outside. Her parents weren't due home, but someone was coming up the stairs fast. Jennifer screamed and the door Artur was blocking crashed open, sending him flying across the kitchen floor.

"Marty!" Jennifer cried. "Oh, thank God!"

Martin decked Artur with one blow. "I had second thoughts about leaving you, *mi hermana*. I didn't want you home alone, so I decided to come back and wait until Mom and Pop got home," Martin said, holding Jennifer in his arms. "We'll call the police now, and it'll all be over."

Jennifer stared at the boy lying on the floor with sadness and fear mixed inside her.

Chapter 10

Jennifer couldn't sleep all night. The rumors Alma heard about the police finding Santiago's body were not confirmed yet. Artur had been taken away to the place he dreaded most—the jail. If he went on trial for hurting Santiago, Jennifer knew she would have to testify. Her words would be the ones that would destroy the second son of that tragic family.

Jennifer rose from bed around eleven and went to the window she had been standing at that terrible night. The moon now hid behind the clouds. When it emerged it would be a sliver, a quarter, then finally a half moon. Tears ran down Jennifer's face as she stared down into the street. And then, suddenly, her blood turned icy cold. A blue sedan cruised slowly under a street light.

Jennifer ran to her parents bedroom. "Dad, hurry, get the car," she said.

"At this hour?" Dad asked. He'd been reading in bed.

"Please!" Jennifer cried with such urgency that her father threw down his book. Jennifer tossed him the car keys and, still wearing his bathrobe, he hurried down the stairs ahead of Jennifer. They both climbed into the family car. Jennifer directed her father onto Hawthorne Street. "Where are we going?" he asked.

"Turn left," Jennifer commanded. They were on 22nd Avenue when Jennifer saw the blue sedan again. They kept the car in sight as it left the brightly lit city and reached the outskirts. When the blue sedan turned into a small motel, Jennifer told her father to follow.

"What's going on?" Jennifer's father asked.

Jennifer got out of the car at Room 16 and pounded with both fists on the door. In a few minutes the door opened. "I knew it was you!" Jennifer screamed at Santiago Velasquez.

He stood there grinning. "Had you all going, didn't I? Did Artur really sweat? I saw you looking out the window, Jennifer, so I figured you'd tell on him."

"Lots of people thought you were dead," Jennifer's father said sharply. "Where the devil have you been?"

Santiago grinned again. "I nicked my hand real bad ... really ticked me off that now I'd miss playing basketball—all because of that little creep Sandoval. And, well, my Dad is out of town anyway, and so I thought it might be fun playing dead for a while."

Jennifer looked at the boy with disgust. "You make me sick, Santiago Velasquez, and pretty soon you're gonna be sorry about what you did!" she said.

Jennifer was at school when she heard that Santiago had been suspended from the basketball team for the season. Artur was released in time to play in next Friday's game, and this time Jennifer agreed to go for pizza with him.

"I'm sorry my brother punched you, Artur," Jennifer said. "He feels bad about it. He wishes he could have punched Santiago instead."

Artur smiled. "It's okay. You found where that bum Santiago was hiding out. That more than makes up for it, Jennifer. In fact, I think I owe you a string of pearls."

Jennifer giggled. "No. You just have to come to our house and make *pollo encasuela con legumbres* again and this time we'll all celebrate!" she said.